John Zephaniah Holwell

An Address from John Zephaniah Holwell

John Zephaniah Holwell

An Address from John Zephaniah Holwell

ISBN/EAN: 9783337375164

Printed in Europe, USA, Canada, Australia, Japan

Cover: Foto ©Andreas Hilbeck / pixelio.de

More available books at **www.hansebooks.com**

AN
ADDRESS

FROM

JOHN ZEPHANIAH HOLWELL, Esq;

TO

LUKE SCRAFTON, Esq;

In reply to his Pamphlet, intitled,

OBSERVATIONS

ON

Mr. VANSITTART's NARRATIVE.

LONDON:

Printed for T. BECKET and P. A. DE HONDT, near
Surry-Street, in the Strand. MDCCLXVII.

[PRICE ONE SHILLING.]

To LUKE SCRAFTON, Esq;

SIR!

I CONFESS my obligation to you for your letter, without date, received yesterday, and accompanied by a printed pamphlet, entitled, "Observations on Mr. VANSITTART's Narrative," of which you avow yourself the author. Sorry I am that this singular production of yours did not come to my hands sooner; for if it had, be assured, Sir, you should not so long have imposed on the world, nor on the *circle of your own acquaintance,* without incurring the just chastisement of my pen, in return for the many flagrant calumnies, and injurious insinuations it contains against me. In all probability, you are pluming yourself with the thoughts that its poisonous effects have already answered your worst purposes, and wrought sufficiently upon the minds of others, before an op-

B   portunity

portunity was given me of replying to it. Herein you may be miftaken; for thinking people are too confiderate to determine on one fide of the queftion, without giving a candid hearing to the other.

I fhall not follow the unfair example you have fet me, of picking out fuch paffages only of my Memorial and letters as feem to make beft for your purpofe : the Public fhall have your whole Epiftle to me verbatim before them; while I take the liberty of commenting firft upon it, and afterwards of refuting the mifreprefentations and falfehoods contained in the pamphlet itfelf.

Letter from Mr. SCRAFTON to Mr. HOLWELL.

SIR!

" Although I am not the author of the Ob-
" server, to which you have replied, I am of the
" accompanying Pamphlet, which never was pu-
" blifhed, nor defigned to be circulated, had not
" Mr. VANSITTART thought fit to take upon him
" the character of head of a party, in oppo-
" fition

" fition to the prefent Directors: his activity in
" that character, and fome circumftances which
" happened in April laft, made it neceffary, for
" my own juftification among the circle of my own
" acquaintance, to make fome obfervations on
" Mr. VANSITTART's publication ; this led me
" to difprove your Memorial, which my particu-
" lar connection with Lord CLIVE enabled me to
" do.

" When you fent me one of your Hiftorical
" Events, I then wrote you, that I reprefented
" your Memorial as falfe, or mifreprefented, in
" every inftance; as alfo your Account of the
" revenues, which has been productive of much
" mifchief to the Company, and is fo totally falfe,
" that befides the grofs fum of eleven crore, be-
" ing eight and a half crore more than the real
" fact; the items it is compofed of are ridicu-
" loufly falfe.—You rate the city of DACCA at two
" crore.——The whole province, city included,
" is but twenty-five laacks—the cuftoms of the
" city, I dare fay, do not pafs 40,000 rupees. As
" you have thought fit to publifh thofe things to

B 2   " the

" the world, you muft take the confequence of
" having gone on fuch wrong informations.

" I am, Sir, &c.

" CORNER of UPPER-BROOK-
" STREET, GROSVENOR-SQUARE."

I cannot avoid looking upon the firft paragraph
of your letter as an aukward apology, flowing from
confcious fhame for your unprovoked attacks on
the veracity of my Publications. What thofe
circumftances were, which made it neceffary for
your own juftification to infult Mr. VANSITTART,
I am an utter ftranger to : but where was the neceffity, I afk, of wounding that gentleman through
my fides ? and in fuch a virulent manner too, that
your pamphlet would much more confiftently bear
the title of *An envenomed Invective againft Mr.
HOLWELL's Conduct and Government*, than that which
is prefixed to it ; and can you think, Sir, that the
Public is fo fhort-fighted as not to fee through
your weak plea of neceffity for difproving my Memorial ? Alas ! Sir, the caufe which ftirred your
gall

gall againſt me is too recent to be already forgot; and the ſpite and premeditated malice which creeps through the whole of your performance, ſtrongly mark the motives that dictated it, as I will maniꞏ feſt when it comes under my particular conſideration: therefore you ſhould have been more careful that you ſtood upon good ground before you began the aſſault, although ſupported by your boaſted *particular connection* with Lord Clive,

I come now to your ſecond paragraph; the whole of which is a rude undigeſted attack upon my Eſtimate of the real value of the Bengall Provinces. Whether you are, or are not, the author of the East India Observer, Nº 6. and 7. it is now pretty plain that paper has been broached under your *moſt ſignificant* auſpices, and that you have ſupplied the author with his ſcandalous anecdotes and materials; becauſe the ſame charges are laid againſt me in that paper, Nº 6. and nearly in the ſame words as they ſtand in your pamphlet: and in Nº 7. about the time that you was penning your ſecond paragraph to me, the Anonymous Author, in reply to my East India Observer Extraordinary, although foreign to his ſubject, aims a ſtroke at my eſtimate

of

of the revenues to the fame purport as yours.
But that hireling is beneath my further notice:
and had I received the fmalleft intimation that
fuch a pamphlet as yours had been exifting and
circulated, that Tool would never have been the
object of my Pen. Miftake me not, Sir, nor
draw a conclufion from thence, that I think you
an object more worthy of it : the vindication of
my own character, from your now avowed afperfions, obliges me to wipe them off.—But to proceed with your fecond paragraph.

I well remember, Sir, that on the firft publication of my HISTORICAL EVENTS, I had the honour
of your fuperficial remarks on my eftimates, and
a menace, that you intended to publifh a refutation of them and my Memorial, and of every
thing elfe that I had publifhed in my Vindication.
——You well remember too, how I treated that
menace; and told you, if you had wifdom, you
would let it alone : which, it feems, you had not.
On hearing you had reprefented to the Court of
Directors my Eftimates of the real value of the BEN-
GALL Provinces as utterly falfe and without foundation, I was neceffitated to explain myfelf, and fupport

my

my affertions in a letter to the Court of Directors from Bath; which letter I publifhed as a Supplement to the fecond edition of the firft part of my HISTORICAL EVENTS, a ftep I fhould not have taken, had the Court of Directors had the civility to acknowledge the receipt of it: to that letter I beg leave to refer the candid Public; and although it does not fuit with your purpofe to underftand me, it will be very obvious to the world, that my calculations arofe not from the amount of what was, or had been actually and openly brought to account, but from the real produce and annual value of the lands and revenues of the provinces, which are funk, embezzled, and diffipated in various fhapes, and are not brought to the credit of the government at all. By analogous reafoning on facts lying before the Court of Directors, I founded my affertion, that the BENGALL Provinces would, on a ftrict general fcrutiny and reform in the rents and revenues, and a new, although favourable meafurement of the lands, produce annually rather above than under elevern Khorore.——Mr. Johnfton's fenfible and fpirited letter to the Proprietors, affords the ftrongeft fupport to my analogous reafoning; for by that

Gentle-

Gentleman's indefatigable labours it appears;
(page 9. of his letter) that in the diftrict of
BURDWAN only there were 412,491 acres of land
lopt from the farms, to the annual value of
116,727 *l.*——That my affertion of eleven khorore
could bear no allufion to the known public revenues as rated upon the Emperor's books, but on
the contrary to the actual produce and intrinfic
value of the provinces, on a general reform, is
obvious from the conftant tenor and bent of my
arguments; for when I have occafionally mentioned the ftanding revenues, I have rather under-
valued than over-rated them, particularly page
51 of INDIA Tracts, publifhed February 1764, by
BECKET, where (in my Addrefs to the Proprietors) urging my reafons againft the commander in
chief of the troops having a vote in the committee or council, I conclude the paragraph in
the following words: " There will ever be one
" fet of political views in the cabinet, and another
" in the camp; and this muft inevitably be the
" cafe; had it not been fo, you would, in the
" month of May or June, 1760, have been your-
" felves SUBAS of BENGALL, and now in poffef-
" fion of between *two and three millions fterling per*

I   " *annum.*"

" *annum*." Here I fpoke without any retrofpect
to the knowledge and conviction I then had of
the intrinfic worth of the country.—Lord CLIVE,
in his letter to the Proprietors, publifhed the fame
year, exceeds me by a million fterling; for his
Lordfhip (page 16.) fpeaking of SURAJUD Dow-
LA, fays,———" His death foon followed, and
" MEER JAFFIER was in a few days in poffeffion
" of the government, and of a revenue of three
" millions and a half fterling."——Mr. Johnfton
exceeds his Lordfhip (page 16 of his letter
before referred to :) fpeaking of the treaty
with the young NABOB, fucceffor to MHIR JAF-
FIER, he fays, " There remained with him, after
" the feveral allowances to be ftipulated in favour
" of the company, a revenue of about two and
" a half millions fterling." To this fum, if we
add the monthly allowance of five lack, to be
paid by the NABOB in lieu of troops, amounting
annually to 812,000, the revenues of BURDC-
MAAN, CHITTYGONG, and MIDNAPORE, ceded by
COSSIM ALY KHAN, eftimated, the loweft, at
600,000 *l.* the twenty-four Purgunnahs, ceded by

JAFFIER

JAFFIER KHAN, eftimated at 100,000 *l.* and Lord CLIVE's Jaggier (being the rents only of the 24 Purgunnahs) at 30,000 l. and the ZEMINDAARY of CALCUTTA at 16,000 l. we fhall find the ftated public revenues of the provinces amount to 4,058,000 *l. Sterling per annum,* which I believe is neareft the truth.—I advance thefe inftances in proof of my affertion, that I rather under-rated than over-valued the ftated public revenues of the provinces; and in proof alfo that when I pronounced the annual value of them to be 11 Khorore, I could neither mean nor allude to thofe (collected upon the prefent mode) but what they would with a moral certainty produce upon an eafy detection of immenfe frauds, when the country was under a BRITISH government. On this pofition alone I ftaked my *credit* and *veracity,* and would as readily ftake my head as a forfeiture on the iffue, if ever my plan of a general fcrutiny and reform throughout the provinces is carried into faithful execution.—Regarding what you fay of DACCA, it is a known fact that the frauds and diffipations in

the

the lands and revenues of that diftrict are more notorious than in any other part of the provinces.

You are pleafed to allege, Sir, " that my ac- " count of the revenues has been productive of " much mifchief to the Company :"—in the name of common fenfe, what mifchief could accrue to the Company from having their eyes opened, that they might view in profpect the real value of the pro- mifed land they were entitled to poffefs ?

Thus much I have thought neceffary to fay in anfwer to your letter. I fhall now proceed to your pamphlet, avoiding, as much as I can, a repetition of the pleas urged in my defence againft the ano- nymous author of the East India Obferver, N.º 6, in my East India Obferver extraordinary, publifhed the 28th December laft, which I intreat the public will do me the honor of keeping in their view.

C 2   The

The mean incenfe offered to Lord CLIVE in the firſt pages of your " Obſervations on Mr. VAN-" SITTART's Narrative," ſhould have drawn no animadverſion from me, had you not laboured to exalt his Lordſhip's character at the expence of truth; if by *his fucceffor* you meant me.—Page 6 of your pamphlet, you are pleaſed to ſay (in defence of a charge laid againſt his Lordſhip by Mr. VANSITTART) " it did not enter into Lord CLIVE's " computation, that *his fucceffor* ſhould run up the " expence to almoſt double that ſum; nor could " he who had defeated the army of SURAJAH " DOWLA with three thouſand men, conceive the " ENGLISH ſhould ever keep up an army of fifteen " thouſand!"—Let it in the firſt place be remem-bered, that howſoever happy in its conſequences the *defeat at* PLASSEY proved to individual ſuffer-ers, the means by which it was obtained ſhould rather be forgot, nor ſhould you blazon that defeat with the ſemblance of a military act of prowefs, which was ſolely owing to the treaſon and treachery

of

of ROYDULLOB and MHIR JAFFIER, two of SU-
RAJAH DOWLA's generals, the higheſt in office, as
well as in the confidence of their maſter ; thus be-
trayed, no glory would have been reflected on our
arms, had the defeat been atchieved with one fourth
of the men then under Lord CLIVE's command.——
His Lordſhip's eſtabliſhed character of a brave
officer ſtands not in need of any falſe luſtre to be
caſt upon it ; nor will you, I believe, Sir, receive
his thanks for this wanton folly of your pen.———
Reſpecting your unwarranted inſinuation againſt
bis ſucceſſor in the above quotation, it was incumbent on you to have examined the general returns
of the troops regularly tranſmitted to the court of
Directors, and by comparing the general return de-
livered to me the 9th of February, 1760, with ſub-
ſequent ones, you would have ſeen there was no
augmentation of the troops worth notice during the
term of my government, nor of expence neither,
beyond what the exigences of the then very com-
plicated nature of the ſervice required.

In

In page 8th of your pamphlet, you are pleafed to draw a conclufion in the following words: " Hence arofe the diftreffes of the SUBAH, and the " Company; the provinces affigned to the Com- " pany became the feat of war."——Now, Sir, you could have no motive for this conclufion, but the very obvious unworthy one of cafting an odium on the conduct of Colonel CAILLAUD, the then commander in chief of the troops, which you with- out any juft foundation had been labouring at in your two preceding paragraphs, page 7.——That the enemy was not purfued after the action of SEER- POOR, on the 23d February, 1760, was an accufa- tion from which Colonel CAILLAUD moft clearly exculpated himfelf. His purfuit could have an- fwered no falutary end without cavalry, which was abfolutely refufed him by the young NABOB, al- though folicited for that purpofe, in the moft pref- fing terms. In place of that, or of immediately joining our forces, he fhut himfelf in PATNA, until the 29th of February, on pretence of curing wounds

which

which a boy of ten years old would have been ashamed to own as such.——The SHAW ZADAH did not make his appearance in the BURDWAN country before the 15th or 16th of March, whereas Colonel CLIVE could hardly have cleared the BENGAL river, before SUBUT and his MAHARATTORS had poffeffed themfelves of MIDNAPOOR and other parts of the skirts of the BURDWAN; fo that in fact it was at *this time* that the lands affigned to the company firft became the feat of war, at leaft in all its effects; for fuch was the confufion, that a ftop was put to all commerce on the bare alarm of SUBUT's advance. Thefe deftructive confequences might have been eafily prevented, had the SOUBAH exerted the fmalleft degree of courage, or hearkened to my preffing inftances to him on that occafion; for inftead of ordering his troops (joined to a ftrong detachment of ours) under the command of his fon in law COSSIM ALI KHAN, to march to the fouthward, and drive SUBUT out of the country, his pufillanimous fears prompted him to direct their

march

march to CUTWAH and the city; by which unfortunate meafure the BURDWAN country was aban-
doned and left a prey to SUBUT and his MAHA-
RATTORS, to the irreparable difgrace of the Sou-
BAH's government, and damage of the Company.
But this was not the only ill confequence which followed that meafure; for SUBUT gained ftrength
and footing daily in the country, and afterwards,
by a junction with the BIERBOHEEN RAJAH, faci-
litated the SHAW ZADDAH's entrance into BURDO-
MAAN: whereas, had SUBUT been vigoroufly op-
pofed in the beginning, and driven back, that diftrict would have been freed from troubles; the re-
ceipts of our TUNKA's would have been uninter-
rupted, and the SHAW ZADDA would have had no
encouragement to have made that fudden march to
the fouthward, as we were afterwards well informed
his chief incitement to that ftep, was the diverfion
which would be made in his favour by the MAHA-
RATTORS.—On the whole, Sir, I have made it
clearly appear, that the diftreffes of the SOUBAH and

the

the Company had their rife in BURDWAN, above
a month earlier than the period you affign for
them, and from a very different caufe, to wit, the
daftardly conduct only of your hero MHIR JAF-
FIER; and, I repeat it, you could have had no motive for *the conclufion* before quoted, but that unworthy one of throwing a reflection on Colonel
CAILLAUD's conduct.

I come now, Sir, to your formal attack upon
myfelf and government, beginning at page the 8th
of your pamphlet; how well you have acquitted
yourfelf in the execution, and how much to your
credit, will appear in the fequel to *the circle of your
own acquaintance* and the public.

You begin your affault in the words following.
" Throughout the whole of Mr. HOLWELL's go-
" vernment, we may trace the defign of a revo-
" lution upon a bare examination, of what he
" thought fit to publifh." In proof of this affertion, you quote part of my letter to Colonel
CAILLAUD of the 11th of March 1760, and a fcrap

D   of

of mine of the 21ft of the fame month to Mr.
HASTINGS. The firft of thefe quotations flatly
contradicts your affertion; for there, I fay, " we
" muft however fupport him and his government
" as long as we poffibly can, without involving
" ourfelves and our employers in his ruin;" if this
implied a defigned revolution, words have no
meaning. —— I wrote to Mr. HASTINGS in the
fame ftrain, 'tis true; but had you been either candid or juft in your quotations or reflections, you
would have given the public the laft paragraph of
Colonel CAILLAUD's letter to me, of the 27th of
February, to which mine was a reply, as well as
thofe parts of mine which introduced the lines you
difingenuoufly quote, and alfo the fentence immediately preceding that which you recite from
my letter to Mr. HASTINGS. From thefe it would
have glaringly appeared, that inevitable ruin muft
attend the SUBAH and his government, without a
change and reform in his conduct and politics,
which we had no reafon to hope: and therefore I
fhould have been little worthy the charge I then
poffeffed, had I fuffered my employers and the
country to be involved in his ruin; and this neceffary and juft precaution you are pleafed to conftrue
into a premeditated defign of a revolution, a charge

4   which

which nothing but your own little malicious genius could poffibly have fuggefted to my prejudice: for the paffage, if difcuffed with candor and fairnefs, rather makes my conduct meritorious, than liable to cenfure.——You clofe page the 8th with faying, " and in the fame letter he accufes the " SUBAH of engaging in a feparate correfpondence " with the SHAZADA."—And at the foot of the page you add a falfe note of reference to miflead the public, and fend them a wild goofe chace that you might more fecurely efcape detection. Your note fays, " Vide HOLWELL's Vindication, pub-" lifhed by BECKET in 1760 ;" whereas the correfpondence you make your quotations and remarks from, was publifhed by BECKET in 1764, under the title of *India Tracts*, by Mr. HOLWELL and his friends; and the *Vindication* which your fpurious note refers to (publifhed likewife in 1764) was purely a defence of his character, (againft an anonymous pamphlet put forth under the title of " Reflections on the prefent ftate of our EAST IN-" DIA affairs,") in which you knew there was not a fyllable contained of the correfpondence with Colonel CAILLAUD or Mr. HASTINGS, which is now the fubject of your remarks.—— Blufh therefore, Sir, at a procedure fo unworthy. ——

But

But once more to take up the thread of your pamphlet, which opens a fresh charge against me, and intimates my having falsely accused the SUBAH of a separate correspondence with the SHAW ZADDA; this you lay as a corroborating proof of my *designing a revolution.*

In support of this charge you quote (page 9.) my instructions to Captain· SPEARS; and, lower, you say, I " come nearer to the point." In my letter to Col. CAILLAUD of the 7th of April, part of which you also quote, (erroneously, or more likely intentionally, giving it a place in page 31 of my correspondence, instead of page 28.) and at the close of your quotation, page 10. you make the following profound remark. " This proves that
" Mr. HOLWELL was carrying on a correspon-
" dence with the SHAW ZADDA at the very time
" our forces were acting against him in the field;
" at the very time he is imputing it as a crime to
" the SUBAH, that he is engaged in the like cor-
" respondence; his own correspondence he ac-
" knowledges; but that of the SUBAH is attended
" with no such proof: for the following is an ex-
" tract of the answer from Colonel CAILLAUD,"
dated 15 April 1760, from DIGNAGUR.——Pray, Sir,

Sir, how does this prove Mr. HOLWELL's correspondence with the SHAW ZADDA? He did not
write himself to COMGAAR KHAN; he employed
an emiffary to him; if I thought I had fufficient
grounds for giving credit to the intelligence given
me of the SUBAH's *arzjee* to the Prince, was it
not a duty ftrictly incumbent on my truft and fta-
tion to trace out the fact? And had you not moft
unfairly fuppreffed the two laft paragraphs of my
letter of the 7th of April to Colonel CAILLAUD;
(notwithftanding they immediately followed your
quotation) my juft caufes for not doubting of my
information, would have appeared moft manifeft.
But this would have made againft your infinuations.—The paragraphs I allude to are as follow.
" I inclofe you copy of a letter fent the OLD NA-
" BOB by the Colonel, which I dictated to the
" MOONSHEE by his order a few days before his
" departure, on his being informed the NABOB
" intended fending a *meffenger* and *petition* to the
" Prince."

" Whether this" (meaning the copy of the Su-
BAH's *arzjee)* " is a real copy or not, I will not
" fay, though I firmly believe it true; that an
" *arzjee* has been fent is allowed, but if it con-
                                        " tained

" tained not matter detracting or injurious to us,
" why was it fent without being communicated to
" you by MHÍRAN, or to HASTINGS by the
" NABOB?"

In my letter to Colonel CAILLAUD of the 9th
of April 1760, (page 30. of the 2d edition of
INDIA TRACTS, publifhed by BECKET, 1764,) I
conclude with telling him, " I have returned no
" anfwer to the prince's *phirmaund*, but have re-
" plied to COMGAAR's letter, and intimated to
" him that I put no faith in copies, but that if
" he would fend me the SUBAH's original *arzjee*,
" I fhall then be able to form a judgment."——
This, Sir, if your intentions had been fair, you
would have referred the public to, as well as have
recited the purport of my letter to COMGAAR
KHAN, as tranfmitted to the fame gentleman, under date the 24th of April 1760, when you was
remarking from that very letter on fuch parts as
you thought made for your purpofe of detraction,
which, fince you have omitted, I muft lay before
the public as it ftands ; p. 35. of INDIA TRACTS,
(2d edition) " That I had received the *phirmaund*,
" and pitied the Prince's unhappy fituation, and
" misfortunes of his royal houfe ; that he (COM-

" GAAR

" GAAR KHAN) was no ftranger to the *ties and*
" *obligations, which bound us to fupport* MHÎR
" JAFFIER ALÎ KHAN *and his government*; that
" copies amounted to no proof, but that if his
" original *arzdafht* was fent me by the prince,
" I fhould then know what judgment to form
" of it."

The extract of Colonel CAILLAUD's anfwer of
the 15th of April (which you recite to invalidate
the proof of the SUBAH's correfpondence with the
Prince, from the fentiments of Mr. HASTINGS)
is equally difingenuous with all the reft of your quotations and remarks; or you would have fet forth
(or at leaft referred the public to) my arguments
in refutation of thofe fentiments in my letter to
Mr. Haftings of the 20th of April 1760, (p. 34.)
and even the circumftances of my meffengers being plundered at SEARPOOR of their returning difpatches from the Prince, as mentioned in my letter
to Colonel CAILLAUD of the 24th of April, which
you allude to, page 11, were to me a ftrong corroborating proof that the SUBAH's *arzjee* to the
Prince was a truth, and no forgery, as pretended;
but fuppofing the whole of what you call my correfpondence with the Prince was minutely known

to

to the SUBAH, he could not, from the nature of
it, have any cause or foundation for even surmis-
ing, much less "being convinced that a revolution
"was then intended," (as you advance, page 12.)
unless from the self-conviction of his own perfidy,
and apprehension of it's being discovered.— On
the whole, Sir, I do aver, that nothing but a deep
and premeditated malevolence like yours, could
have given the turn to this transaction that you
have done; a transaction that bears not the least
semblance of my engaging in any correspondence
with the SHAW ZADDA, that tended in any shape
to injure the SUBAH or his government, (but the
very reverse) or that spoke *my design of a revolution,*
which this charge is impotently brought forth to
support; my intelligence originally was from a
quarter I could not suspect of deceiving me. My
duty to my employers, to myself, to the country,
the perilous situation of our troops, and of our
affairs in general, if such a wicked negotiation had
taken effect, were all causes sufficiently alarm-
ing to stimulate my enquiry into the truth of it;
and this enquiry was prosecuted with all the deli-
cacy respecting the SUBAH's character, that the
nature of the thing could possibly admit of.

From

From Colonel Caillaud's 2d paragraph of his letter to me of the 15th of April, (you took care, Sir, only to quote the first) it appeared to me that the Subah and his son had at that time a double game to play, either to make their peace with the prince and sacrifice us, or by treachery to get their lawful sovereign into their hands and murder him; I have a voucher by me that fully proves the latter; then why should we have the least doubt of his being capable of perpetrating the former? —" One Comdarry, duan to Comgaar Khan, engaged by letter to the Subah to put the Prince into his hands or cut him off, if the Nabob would agree to give him a lack of rupees, and the command of Comgaar Khan's country; these proposals being agreed to, they were transmitted to Comdarry under the hands and seals of the two Nabobs, the 16th of April 1760, at night, from the camp at Dignagore, when the two armies were not far distant from each other." This negotiation needs no comment——As I had an early conviction of the badness of the Subah's heart, it was the duty of my post ever to be upon my guard against him, and therefore it was, that I thought it necessary to give the precautionary instructions to Captain Spears, which you recite, page 9. as evidence of my *designed revolution.*

E   You

You are pleafed to fay in page 12. " Mr. Hol-
" well puts the queftion more plainly to Mr.
" Caillaud."——If you mean any thing by *put-
ting the queftion,* I fuppofe it is the queftion of a
revolution, although in truth the quotation you
make from my letter of the 24th of May, contains no queftion at all, but ftates matters of fact
only ; and with your ufual difingenuity, you fink
the clofe of my preceding paragraph, by which it
would exprefsly appear, that in the quotation you
make as *fingly mine,* I was not only tranfmitting to
the Colonel my own fentiments, but the dictates
of the fecret Committee——it is from thence evident it fuited your genius and intention better
to calumniate me alone : — But fince in your quotation, page 12. you have thought proper to ftop
in the middle of my paragraph, I will take it up
where you break off. —— " The more we fee of
" this government, the more is verified your own
" juft obfervation at your firft knowledge of it,
" *that it is rotten to the core* ; what then can be ex-
" pected from a fyftem rotten to the very heart
" of it?——In every fenfe ruin muft attend the
" family, in fpite of our efforts to fave them, and
" we muft as affuredly be partakers in a lefs or
" greater degree thereof ; to fay nothing of our

2   " drawing

" drawing our fwords in fupport of fuch a fyftem,
" againft the legal, though unfortunate, Prince
" of the country, from whom every advantage
" and emolument we can wifh for the Company,
" is tendered to us without limitation." ———
Thefe, Sir, you know were the fentiments of the
Committee as well as my own; therefore, why did
you give them to the public as fingly mine?———
Here I confefs our defign and wifh for the firft
time was to diveft this family of the government,
as the fupporting them longer became utterly incompatible with the well-being of the Company
and the country, as fufficiently appears from the
deep diftreffes of both, fet forth without the fmalleft
exaggeration.

Pages 13 and 14 of your pamphlet you make
a long quotation from Colonel CAILLAUD's anfwer
(to mine of the 24th of May) which you think
moft exactly makes for your purpofe, becaufe it
contains the Colonel's reafons, and diffent to our
making a revolution *in favour of any other perfon*;
———from a bare glance on the laft quotation, from
my letter of the 24th of May, and the Colonel's
anfwer, it is moft evident he mifunderftood (I will
not fay defignedly) the meaning and intentions of

E 2   the

the felect committee, as there is not a word in the letter he was anfwering, that bore the leaft intimation of our having a wifh to transfer the Subahfhip to *any other perfon* in the provinces. ——Had the fpirit of honor and candor poffeffed you, (of which you give me caufe to fay you have not a grain) you would have given the public my explanation of this matter, as it ftands in my reply to the Colonel, under date 14th June 1760, (page 51. INDIA TRACTS) which is as follows.——

" Had it ever been my wifh or intention to
" have taken our fupport from the prefent NA-
" BOB, and transfer it to any other, your arguments
" in that cafe would have all the weight with me
" they fo greatly merit; but I think on the repre-
" fentations in mine to you, and the copy of mine
" to Mr. AMYATT, you will fee that was not my
" aim, for I concur minutely with your objections
" to fuch a ftep, and am very clear we fhould not
" mend our fituation by a revolution in favour of
" any other, who would, as you truly obferve,
" prove as bad as the prefent, and probably worfe;
" but my views for the Company went much
" higher. — That the country will never be in a
" fettled peaceful ftate, whilft this family is at the
" head

" head of it, is a pofition I lay down as inconteft-
" able; and that until the country enjoys that
" ftate, the Company's affairs muft be daily ap-
" proaching to certain ruin; I therefore judge we
" could never be poffeffed of a more favourable
" opportunity to carry into execution what muft
" be done, I plainly fee, one time or other, (if
" the Company have ever a fecure footing in the
" provinces) to wit, take this country into their
" own hands, limiting ourfelves to the province
" of Bengal only, or extending our views to thofe
" of BAHAAR and ORIXA, as on future debate
" might be thought moft eligible.—The fituation
" of the Prince at prefent is fuch, that I am fure
" he would readily and heartily hearken to any
" overture from us, and without hefitation grant a
" phirmaund, appointing the Company perpetual
" SUBAHS of the province; his two phirmaunds
" to me, as I before advifed you, offered a carte
" blanche for the Company, and I dare fay that
" to you was of the fame tenor."—— In a note to
page 10, you fay the Colonel denied his having
received any Phirmaund from the Prince: where
he denies this I know not; I can only aver, fo he
advifed the felect Committee, and promifed to
fend them a copy, which he never did; and it is
moft

moſt improbable that I ſhould refer to it, as I have
done in my reply of the 14th of June, if no
ſuch advice had been ſent. — Although it was my
ſincere opinion that there was a neceſſity for diveſt-
ing this family of the government, yet it is plain
I was not of opinion that they ſhould be abandon-
ed, how little ſoever they merited conſideration;
for in my laſt mentioned letter, page 53, I medi-
tate a ſtipulation, that Mhîr Jaffier and his ſon
ſhould be preferred *to ſome conſiderable poſts* under
the Prince, in caſe we entered into a treaty with
him for the Subahdary of the provinces. All that
I think neceſſary to add touching your long quotation from Colonel Caillaud's anſwer, is to refer
the public to the whole of my reply of the 14th
of June, and my remarks on the Colonel's letter,
(page 50 and 51 of India Tracts.)

Page 14 of your pamphlet, you are pleaſed to
ſay, with as little truth as manners, " July 1,
" Mr. Holwell *invents a new calumny* againſt the
" Subah ſtill more improbable than any, viz.
" that he is negotiating for twenty-five thouſand
" Morattors to enter his country."—To clear
myſelf from this baſe aſperſion, (which merits a
barſher name) and to expoſe your talent at ſlander,
muſt

muſt employ more lines than I at preſent wiſh, (could it be avoided) becauſe I am impatient to come to your bungling diſſection of my Memorial.

About the middle of June I firſt received advice from Mr. HASTINGS, the Company's Reſident at MORADBAAG, of a prevailing report, that the SU-BAH was negotiating a treaty with the MAHARAT-TORS, and on the 21ſt of the ſame month I received a letter from the above-mentioned gentleman, in which was the following paragraph.——
" The NABOB ſeems much elated by this victory,
" (over CUDDEIM HOSSEYN KHAN) but more ſo by
" the late advices from DEHLI, which mention
" that the ABDALLEE is obliged to retreat before
" the VIZÎR, who has gained ſome conſiderable
" advantages over him : the particulars have not
" come to my knowledge, but the NABOB has
" received a letter from the VIZÎR to this purpoſe,
" and has had the news confirmed to him. The
" VIZÎR's letter, I am told, the NABOB has an-
" ſwered, and requeſted that 25 or 30,000 MAH-
" RATTORS may be ſent to his aſſiſtance, in order
" to drive out the SHAW ZADDA ; and at the ſame
" time MAUSALOODOE MHAMUT KHAN, and the
" two MAHRATTOR VAKÎLS have received their
                                        " diſmiſ-

" difmiffion, the firft to remain at CUTTACK,
" the latter to proceed to SITANAGUR, to forward
" by their prefence this motion of the NABOB's."
——I had but juft received this intelligence from
our refident, when a meffage was fent me from
ROY DOOLUB, that he defired leave to pay me a
vifit; he came and brought RAJARAM HARKA-
RAH with him. The purpofe of this vifit was to
communicate feveral letters they had received the
preceding night from their agents at the SUBAH's
Court, all relative to the ftep the SUBAH had
taken of foliciting a body of MAHARATTOR troops
from the VIZIR, and the particular treaty he was
entering into with the MAHARATTORS in confequence of his requeft to the VIZIR.——Thefe informations I laid before the members of the felect
committee, and it was refolved that they fhould
be tranfmitted to the abfent members, Meffrs.
AMYATT and CAILLAUD, the firft time I had occafion to addrefs them; but that Mr. HASTINGS
fhould be wrote to immediately, which I did, in
the terms following.

June 30, 1760.
" The NABOB's whole conduct put together leaves
" us little room to doubt the truth of your infor-
" ma-

" mation, (touching the MAHARATTOR treaty) his
" fecreting from us his allies, (who at this very
" juncture are faving his throat from being cut)
" a treaty of fuch importance to us, and his coun-
" try, pretty plainly fhews his aim and refolu-
" tion of being independant of us at any rate;
" his fcheme of being fo by means of his friends
" the Dutch, he finds there can be no firm
" reliance on, but rather than not carry his point,
" he will throw himfelf into the hands of a race
" of people, to whom his country, government,
" and family will in the end fall a facrifice.———
" Unlefs independence be his ruling motive to
" this infatuated meafure, the world must be
" at a lofs to divine what motive he can be fway-
" ed by: the pretence of calling in 25 or
" 30,000 MAHARATTORS to drive the SHAW
" ZADDA out of the country, is the moft bare-
" faced one imaginable, and he might as well
" openly declare his fecret councils tend to
" drive us out, as foon as he thinks he has the
" power."

" If the treaty with the MAHARATTORS has
" any real foundation, it has proceeded, on one
" hand, from the art and influence of MAUSAU-

F   " LOODEE

" LOODEE MAHMUT KHAN; and on the other,
" from the weakneſs, cowardice, and fears of the
" NABOB, which are ever kept awake by the ver-
" min about him, who inculcate, without ceaſ-
" ing, that he has every thing to fear from us
" only; however, be this as it may, it is highly
" incumbent on you to get, if poſſible, at the
" bottom of this treaty with the MAHARATTORS,
" and give me, without loſs of time, the moſt au-
" thentic evidence of the truth of it, which you
" can poſſibly obtain: —— For I conceive our
" very being depends upon ſapping the founda-
" tion of this union, and upon preventing, or
" overturning every ſuperſtructure that can be
" raiſed from it. Was the NABOB's aim at inde-
" pendence only, I think its conſequence could
" not much affect us; but if once thoſe locuſts
" are introduced, and gain a footing, adieu to
" the currency of trade, and then, what be-
" comes of the 'Company and Colony? I am,
" &c."—— An occaſion offered to tranſmit the
particulars to Mr. AMYATT the 1ſt July, and
to the Colonel the 3d,—— referring him to Mr.
AMYATT's of the 1ſt.—— Prior to the diſpatch of
Mr. AMYATT's, I had intelligence that the SU-
BAH had dropped his projected treaty, on hearing

ing that I was informed of it, and the fuppreffion of every overture towards it had been fo effectual, that Mr. Hastings fubfequently wrote, " He " could not find fufficient grounds for the treaty ;" but the folicitation to the Vizir remained inconteftable. What opinion the Public may form of the tranfaction itfelf, is at this time of day immaterial; it is fufficient for me, that I have ftated known facts, which prove, that when you charged me with " *inventing this as a calumny upon* " *the* Subah," you was guilty of a bafe afperfion, which a Gentleman ought to blufh at.

I come now, Sir, to your attack upon my Memorial, page 15, of your pamphlet, which you have been pleafed, more than once, to ftigmatife, as either " *falfe cr mifreprefented in every in-* " *ftance*," with what regard to truth will prefently appear.

The firft charge in my Memorial againft the Subah is, " his attempt to evade the terms of " the treaty :" (what impreffion of my Memorial you have copied from, I know not; but by falfe pointing, and leaving out the monofyllable *and*, you have made fhift to make me fpeak flat non-

fenfe

senfe in part of my second paragraph.——Your quotation runs thus:——" The conditions of the " treaty could not be obtained from the SUBAH, " without, in a manner, being extorted from him " by a thoufand shifts and evasions; &c." whereas, the impression before me (Ind. Tr. p. 8.) runs thus: " The conditions of the treaty could " not be obtained from the SUBAH, without, in " a manner, being extorted from him; *and* by a " thoufand shifts and evasions, &c."

Your remark on this charge allows it in fact; for you fay, " that the SUBAH would willingly " have evaded the payment of a million sterling." Was this a proof of his honefty, even to wish to evade a condition of the treaty he had moft folemnly concluded? You add, " he *faithfully* com-" plied with his treaty;" when? You answer yourself,——when he found Colonel Clive's spirit was not to be trifled with, nor imposed upon; so that you are forced to acknowlege, that one of my *inftances*, at leaft, is neither *false* nor *misreprefented:* but to show, Sir, that your own recital bears harder upon your friend JAFFIER than mine, you will pleafe to revert to your production before me, p. 3 and 4, where you fay, " ROYDULLUB was " a GEN-

" a GENTOO or native INDIAN, who had been
" in high employment under SURAJAH DOWLA,
" and was the only one in the secret of MEER
" JAFFIER's engagements to us, and in conse-
" quence thereof, made very high terms with
" his master, demanding for himself and his bro-
" thers all the highest offices of the state."—And a
very natural consequence it was, and what one trai-
tor might expect from another. Don't you know,
Sir, that ROYDULLUB was not the only one in the
secret ? Don't you also know that there was one
more in the secret, *one* OMYCHUND, whose treat-
ment, on that occasion, caused the deprivation of his
senses and death ? I beg leave to step over the paragraph of your own importance (p. 3.) and proceed
to the next, where you own, that " the SUBAH's
" first object was, how to delay or evade the pay-
" ment of the sums stipulated by treaty for the
" Company, half of which was paid, and the re-
" mainder to be discharged in the course of three
" years.——In this important circumstance, ROY-
" DULLUB manifested so evident a partiality to the
" Company, as, together with the exorbitant
" power lodged in his hands, from the many em-
" ployments, civil and military, with which he
" and his family were intrusted, gave rise to a jea-
                                        " lousy

" lousy which soon produced a crisis, &c." A crisis indeed! for we snatched him and his family out of the hands of your monster, just as the sword was at their throats.——Have I any where exhibited so detestable a picture of your hero as you yourself have in that paragraph? The delay or evasion of the payment (the most pressing and essential article of the treaty) you say, was *his first object*.

The offices possessed by ROYDULLUB, he enjoyed too *by treaty*, as being a partaker in the SUBAH'S treason against his master, and it ought to have been scrupulously observed (for traitors and rogues have a law to themselves;) but no sooner did ROYDULLUB *manifest a partiality for the Company*, than he was to be taken off. —— How prevalent is truth! How came you, Sir, in this *single instance*, spontaneously and unawares, to suffer it to drop from your pen?

Your next attack is on the 3d and 4th paragraphs of my Memorial, where I assert, " the " officers of the revenues became our implacable " enemies on account of the Tunkas (or assign " ment of the Lands) and that consequently a

" party

" party was raifed at the DURBAR, headed by
" MHIRAN the SUBAH's fon, and RAJAH RAAGEE
" BULLOB, &c."——To the firft part of my affertions, your remark, p. 16, fays,—" This is
" without the leaft foundation." To the latter
part you aver, " This is fo very far from being
" true, that this RAJABULLOB did, about this
" time, propofe to Colonel Clive the depofing
" MEER JAFFIER in favour of SURAJAH Dow-
" LA's brother." That the propofal was made, I
will not conteft; becaufe I know the man who pro-
pofed it was capable of acting any double part,
however villainous; but pray, how does this prove
that my affertion againft him and MHIRAN *was
far from true?*——Here, Sir, you was not aware,
that at the time you think you are pointing your
envenom'd fhafts againft me only, you are charg-
ing your friend and patron, Colonel Clive, and
his whole BENGAL Council of the year 1760, as
well as the whole Court of Directors of the year
1764, with uttering and circulating the groffeft
falfhoods.—The preamble of the Memorial tranfmitted to the Court of Directors by Governor Clive
and Council, of the difpute with the Dutch at the
latter end of the year 1759, ftand in nearly the
words following:——" About this time twelve

2   " months

" months (about October or November 1758)
" a *prevailing party at the* NIZAM JAFFIER ALI
". KHAN'S DURBAR, *headed by* MHIRAN *his son,*
" had prejudiced him to look with an evil and
" jealous eye on the power and influence of the
" ENGLISH in the provinces, and taught him to
" think and look upon himself as a cypher, bear-
" ing the name of SUBAH only! From subfe-
" quent concurring circumstances, it must have
" been at that period, and from this cause, that a
" private negotiation was set on foot between the
" NIZAM and the DUTCH; that the latter should
" bring a military force into the provinces to join
" the former, and balance our power and sway.
" The DUTCH, stimulated by envy, &c."—The
Company's printed Memorial to the King, signed
3d February, 1762, after specifying the establish-
ment of the SUBAH, takes up the matter and
sense of the fore-recited preamble, but in other
words,' as follows (p. 9.)

" After all this, and when the peace of the
" country was re-established, and the NIZAM
" quietly settled in that station, some of *the Dutch*
" *factory,* (for we do not mean to impute to all,
" what we believe many disapproved) *envying*
" the

" the reputation and influence of the ENGLISH
" at the NIZAM's Court, and hoping to find their
" private account, in reviving the confusion from
" which those provinces had been so happily ex-
" tricated, *associated with others of the like dispofi-*
" *tion, members of the* NIZAM's *Durbar,* and parti-
" cularly with COJA WAZEED, a confiderable mer-
" chant, whofe enmity to the ENGLISH will
" hereafter be accounted for, endeavoured to
" prejudice the NIZAM and his fon, *to look with*
" *an evil and jealous eye on the* ENGLISH, infinuat-
" ing that *he was a cypher,* bearing the name of
" SUBAH *only,* and that the ENGLISH were aim-
" ing to be SUBAHS of the country, in breach of
" their treaty with him."

" Thefe infinuations, groundlefs as they were,
" (fince had the ENGLISH the defign imputed to
" them, what hindered them from carrying it
" into execution, inftead of fupporting the NIZAM
" in raifing himfelf to that dignity?) had at length,
" being often repeated, fo much effect, that they
" inclined him to liften to their propofals; *one*
" *of which was, that the* DUTCH *were to bring*
" *into the province a military force to join his,* and
" curb a power, which was reprefented as fo dan-

G   " gerous,

" gerous. In confequence of this *private negotia-*
." *tion,* we have reafon to believe difpatches were
" forwarded from CHINSURA to BATAVIA, about
" the latter end of the year 1758, which pro-
." duced the armament in queftion."

(I have made, you fee, my quotations from the
two Memorials extend beyond the prefent matter,
to avoid the neceffity of quoting from them again,
when I come to one of your fubfequent remarks.)

When the 3d and 4th paragraphs of my Memorial are compared *by the circle of your own acquaintance,* and the Public, with that from Governor CLIVE and his Council, and that prefented
by the Court of Directors, in the Name of the
Company, to the King,—where, Sir, will you hide
yourfelf from fhame? What, Sir! let your arrows
fly from the dark fhades of ignorance and malice,
and wound and arraign the veracity of your beft
friends! Lord CLIVE! and many of the refpect-
able members of *the prefent Court of Directors,*
who put their hands to the Memorial to the
King; and for whom you are now an avowed
champion!

You

You next attempt, p. 16 and 17, to invalidate my charge againſt the SUBAH for aſſaſſinating of COJA HADDEE and COSSIM ALI KHAN in 1758, and other officers known to be attached to the intereſt of the ENGLISH; (here let it be remembered, that theſe are the only aſſaſſinations that I produced in *my Memorial)* to refute theſe, or rather to apologize for them, you ſay, p. 16, in your Remarks,—" The men here ſaid to be put " to death for their attachment to us, had no " ſort of connection with us;" not immediately, I grant; but their attachment to our intereſt was known and avowed: cauſe enough, witneſs ROY- DULLUB.——Your firſt apology for the SUBAH'S murder of the firſt named of theſe officers is, that " a month or two before his death, he en- " gaged in a project to introduce the FRENCH " by the means of one MUSTAPHA, &c." This ſeems calculated, not only to extenuate the murder, but appears to be introduced chiefly to afford matter of ſlander againſt Mr. VANSITTART, who, you ſay, " employed this MUSTAPHA as " his agent for his inland trade;" for immediately after, you contradict your firſt apology, and ſay, " The *real cauſe* of the SUBA's diſpleaſure was, " that they, with eleven others, ſet their hands

" to

" to a paper mutually to fupport each other,"
(againſt the known tyranny and cruelty of the father and fon, I fuppofe, if any fuch compact
or affociation did really exiſt;) although it was
known to the world thefe were only pretences;
the true caufes of their death were the SUBAH's
jealoufy of their declared attachment to us, and
a greedy thirſt after their poffeſſions: the fame
might juſtly have been faid regarding the murders of ABDEL ONAB KHAN, and YAR MAHO-
MET, which I fhould have particularized in my
Memorial, if it had. been my intention to in-
flame Mr. VANSITTART againſt the SUBAH's and
MHIRAN's crimes,—as thefe murders were rather
more atrocious and cruel than the others.——The
former was way-laid, and affaſſinated by the Su-
BAH's order, on the ROMNAH, on pretence of a
confpiracy, in March 1760.——The latter was cut
to pieces in the prefence of MHIRAN, in April
1760, becaufe he had been a favourite of SURA-
JUD DOWLA, and was fuppofed to have large poffeſſions.——

Page 17 of your remarks, after having difingenuoufly . feparated my 5th paragraph, and
brought down part of it to the bottom of your
page,

page, you begin a new paragraph, which alters my fenfe; you imply an affertion for me which I never meant, and then profoundly fay, " This " is void of all truth; GOLOMSHAW was no re- " lation of the SUBAH's; they were both offi- " cers in his fervice, and revolted to the SHAW " ZADDA."——When my paragraph is connected together, it runs thus: " To this purpofe (of in- " dependence) COJA HADDEE, and COSSIM ALI " KHAN 1ft and 2d BUXY, were affaffinated in No- " vember and December 1758, after many attempts " on the perfons of RHEIM KHAN, and GOLAM " SHAW his uncle and brother; they were ob- " liged to feek an afylum with the SHAW ZADDA." Whofe uncle and brother could I poffibly mean? COSSIM ALI KHAN was the laft perfon named; and therefore, if you had not defignedly mangled my paragraph, it muft plainly read, RHEIM KHAN *was uncle to* COSSIM ALI, *and* GOLAM SHAW *was his brother*; for I know as well as you that he was no relation to the SUBAH.——Fy! Sir,—thefe are little arts unworthy a man.

In your remark upon my affertion, " *that* ROY- " DULLOB *and his four brothers were profcribed*," you give me and the public a very ftriking proof of

the regard you have for truth; people that de-
light in ftory-telling, they fay, ought to have good
memories.—Page 18, of your Remarks, you fay,
" This profcription was *nothing more* than difmiffing
" them from their employments, and they are
" all alive at this time." Pleafe, Sir, to return
back to the 4th page of this correct and authentic
piece of yours, and fee what words follow your
crifis,—" *And the* Subah's *forces were on the point*
" *of attacking him* (Roydullob) when we finding
" the Subah could not be reconciled to him con-
" formable to our agreement, took him under
" our protection, and fent him to Calcutta."—
Here it is evident from your own words, that
had we not moft critically ftept in, Roydullub
and his brothers would have been *difmiffed from
their employments* with a vengeance!——Why, Sir,
would you thus wantonly provoke me to the neceffity of expofing you?

Your next remark (page 18) regards Omhir
Beg Khan: " This man (you fay) quitted the
" country becaufe he had no confidence in any one
" but Lord Clive," in contradiction to my affertion, that nothing could have preferved him (for
his moft remarkable attachment to the Englifh) but
                                                his

his engaging his word to quit the kingdom.—This I know, that Governor CLIVE was, for some days before OMHIR BEG KHAN's arrival in CALCUTTA, in hourly expectation of hearing that he was cut off by MHIRAN. To the reason for his safety given in my memorial, I believe I might have added the SOUBAH's dread of Colonel CLIVE's severe resentment; for the Colonel highly regarded OMHIR BEG, as did every man in the settlement who had any knowledge of him: I attended the governor on a visit to him a few days before he embarked; he was then in a miserable state of health, and most pathetically lamented the necessity he was reduced to, and that he was not permitted quietly to embrace a death that was inevitable from the nature of his disease.

I come now, Sir, (page 18 and 19) to your laboured apology for the SOUBAH, against my charge of his " introducing by secret negociation the " Dutch armament:"—but why should I arrogate so much to myself as to call it *my charge?* it is the charge of Governor CLIVE and his council; it is the charge of the court of Directors of the year 1764, founded on the honour, faith, and veracity of Governor CLIVE and his council, who must be deemed the only, and competent judges of the

transaction.

transaction:——You say, at the beginning of your apology, " That the whole of this charge amounts " to no more than a suspicion, &c." Is it possible to believe that Governor CLIVE and his council would exhibit a charge of this nature on suspicion only? or that the Company, in their memorial to the King, would have taken it up upon no better evidence?—Does not Mr. BISDOM's letter to the SUBAH (Appendix, N° 6. page 55.) expressly say, " *We sent for the said army in consequence of your di-* " *rections*;" let me add Lord CLIVE's confirmation of the company's memorial in his Lordship's own words; (Appendix, N° 13. page 71.) " This " is to certify, that I have *carefully perused* the an- " nexed memorial of the ENGLISH EAST INDIA " Company to his Majesty, and do *solemnly declare,* " that such of the facts therein mentioned as I was " any ways concerned in, *are truly* stated, and that " *I verily believe* the rest to be so.

" CLIVE."

Here I might repeat the unanswerable argu- ments I had occasion to publish before, in defence of this charge against the SUBAH, but shall con-- tent myself with refering to them only (page 102. of Ind. Tr.)——The whole of your apology
. . (founded

(founded on the conjectural motives that led the SUBAH to introduce another EUROPEAN force to *oppose ours*, that he might preserve the balance of power in his own hands) any one but yourself would surely blush to own; could he "have ex- "preffed a defire" of this kind, without a flagrant breach of the treaty fubfifting between us? but he not only *expreffed*, but carried his defire into execution.———You fay, (page 19.) " that when the " DUTCH armament did arrive, he acted the moft " honourable part imaginable."—You chufe not to account for this change, therefore I will, and take the words of the Company's memorial to the King (page 9.) After fpeaking of the advance of the SHAW ZADDA with a numerous army early in the year 1759, it goes on, " whereupon Governor " CLIVE, not regarding, though well apprifed of " the ingratitude with which the NIZAM was half " inclined to return the obligations conferred on " him, readily marched to PATNA in his defence, " to which he owed his deliverance from a danger " that muft otherwife have overwhelmed him. " This was fuch an inftance of fidelity and attach- " ment on the part of the ENGLISH, as made him " *much afhamed* of having liftened to any infinua- " tions to the contrary."—Here, Sir, for the firft

H   time,

time, I will make a conceſſion to you; that there was a manifeſt change in the mind of the SUBAH between the period he ſtipulated for the introduction of the DUTCH armament, and that of their arrival, I will moſt readily acknowledge. Conſcious ingratitude ſtared him in the face! Vengeance for breach' of his ſolemn treaty with us, hung over him! and I dare ſay, he would have given half his Subaſhip could he have recalled the engagements he had entered into the preceding year: that was impoſſible; ſo he had nothing left for it, but to temporiſe between the two powers, and deceive them both if he could.

You add at the cloſe of your remark (page 19.) that " when the DUTCH commenced hoſtilities, he " ſent his ſon with a body of forces to join us;" but you know, Sir, they never did join us, and you know *the reaſon* why they did not, but that you chuſe to ſupprefs:—This reaſon is manifeſted in Governor CLIVE's and his council's memorial, in nearly the following terms; " On this event (the " DUTCH commencing hoſtilities) we concluded " with the greateſt probability, that the DUTCH " had received intelligence of a rupture between " them and us in EUROPE, or *that they were ſure*

" *of*

" *of the* NIZAM*'s joining them, or of his standing*
" *neuter at least* ; *and having the utmost reason to suf-*
" *pect the* NIZAM*'s whole conduct,* Governor CLIVE
" advised him of the acts of violence the DUTCH
" had committed below, adding, that as they had
" commenced actual war against us, he should
" judge the quarrel now subsisted between them
" and us only, desiring he would desist from send-
" ing his son or any part of his army to our assist-
" ance." Thus it is clear, Governor CLIVE
thought that neither the NIZAM, nor his son, nor
his troops, were at that critical juncture to be
trusted ; and these were likewise the sentiments of
his whole council.

Page 20 contains only one remark of fulsome
adulation, the merit of which (if there is any merit
in it) is not your own ; " Lord CLIVE's rule of con-
" duct was, a rigid regard to all engagements." This
profound anecdote, is obviously advanced as a con-
trast to my conduct, and arose from the following
short paragraph of my memorial, INDIA TRACTS,
page 10.

" The Prince more than once wrote to the Co-
" lonel, offering any terms for the Company and
" himself, on conditions the ENGLISH would quit

" the

" the SUBAH, and join his arms ; but the Colone,
" thinking it *incompatible with our alliance*, gave
" the Prince no encouragement."—Here I might
very juftly have added, that it was alfo *incompatible*
with the recent very high obligations the Colonel
lay under to the SUBAH's generofity, otherwife his
conduct appears unaccountable that he did not de-
pofe the SUBAH after the campaign in 1759, upon
the full conviction he owns he had of his treachery
and breach of the treaty in the negociation for the
DUTCH armament.

I have now followed you, Sir, through all your
dirt and rubbifh, to your laft formal attack, where
you refume the refutation of my charge of the affafli-
nations, fupported, as you think, by the foreign auxi-
liary force of Lord CLIVE's letter and certificate of
fome of thofe people being ftill alive : however, the
murders of COJAH HADDEF, COSSIM ALI KHAN,
ABDEL OHAB KHAN, and YAR MAHOMET, as well
as the intended affaffination of ROYDULLUB, are
ftill uncontefted ; thefe continue fufficient vouchers
of the SUBAH's and his fon's cruelties, and there
is no certificate of the firft named four being
alive pretended *as yet.*——Let us fee, upon a
fair difcuffion, how far your foreign aid will
affect us : in order to which, I will beg leave
to tranfcribe the part of his Lordfhip's letter
which

which you have given us, page 23. " I de-
" fire it may be known, *for the honour of* JAFFIER
ALI KHAN, that the murders afcribed to him *in*
Mr. HOLWELL's *memorial, are cruel afperfions, and*
void of all truth, for they are all now living, *except*
the two laft, who were put to death by MHIRAN,
unknown to his father."—If this letter is genuine,
(of which, in compliment to his Lordfhip, I confefs fome doubt) it is at leaft fomething difficult to
be underftood, although the general tendency of it
is plain enough ; but what does his Lordfhip mean
when he excepts *the two laft* put to death by MHI-
RAN? Mr. HOLWELL's memorial contains but a
charge of *two* murders *firft* and *laft,* and thofe you
have murdered as well as I, and affigned the pretended caufes for their being put to death ; or does
his Lordfhip mean ABDEL OHAB KHAN and YAR
MAHOMET? If fo, between you both you have
authenticated my lift of four affaffinations : or per-
haps he means the two laft of my lift, following Mr.
HASTINGS's letter to me, of the 21ft June, (Ind.
Tr. 2d Ed. page 41.) if fo, we have two more
to add to the affaffination-account *authenticated.*—
In truth, as his Lordfhip's very ill founded attack
on my character is confined folely *to my memorial,* I
am utterly at a lofs to comprehend him ; but you,
Sir, I can perfectly comprehend, and plainly fee
you will ftick at nothing to fatiate your little ma-

2   lice.

lice.—In your remarks, page 22. you think proper
to give the laſt two or three lines of Mr. HAS-
TINGS's letter juſt mentioned, and ſuppreſs all the
foregoing parts as well as my ſhort letter that oc-
caſioned that reply, becauſe you plainly ſaw they
both contained matter tending to my juſtification,
and flattered yourſelf they might not be adverted
to by the public ; this obliges me to tranſcribe
them here.

" To Mr. WARREN HASTINGS.

"SIR,   13 June, 1760.

" *By expreſs yeſterday from* DACCA *we have ad-*
" *vice, that the* SUBAH *had taken off* ALIVERDY's
" *and* SHAW AMET KHAN's BEGUMS.——He ſent
" a JEMMAUTDAAR and 100 horſe, with orders
" to JESSURAUT KHAN (then NABOB of DACCA)
" to carry this bloody ſcheme into execution, with
" ſeparate orders to the JEMMAUTDAAR, in caſe
" JESSURAUT KHAN refuſed obedience : he refuſed
" acting any part in the tragedy, and left it to the
" other, who carried them out by night about two
" miles above the city in a boat, tied weights to
" their legs, and throwed them overboard : they
" ſtruggled for ſome time, and held by the gun-
" wal of the boat, but by ſtrokes on their heads
                                    " with

" with latties (ftaves) and cutting their hands, they
" funk.—Thefe are the acts of the tyger we are
". fupporting and fighting for. I am, Sir, &c."

To this letter Mr. HASTINGS returned the following anfwer, dated MORADBOUGH, 21ft June,
1760, fix days at leaft after the receipt of mine.

" SIR,

" The relation tranfmitted to me, in your letter
" of the 13th, of the murder of the two BEGUMS;
" filled me with horror and aftonifhment; but how
" were thofe fenfations increafed, when I was told
" *that not only the two wretched fufferers abovemen-*
" *tioned, but the whole family, to the number of nine*
" *perfons, had undergone the fame fate.* I will not
" mention their names until I have undoubted
" proofs of the truth of my intelligence, which I
" wifh (though I cannot expect it) I may find not
" fo bad at laft *as is reprefented to me.* How this
" circumftance escaped my knowledge, I know
" not; it was not indeed an event to be learned
" from inquiry; and poffibly the infamy of the
" fact might have made my friends who were in
" the fecret neglect to fpeak to me on a fubject,
" which, from our particular connections with the
" NABOB,

" NABOB, and his intire dependence on our power,
" *could not but reflect dishonour on the* ENGLISH *name.*
" I have hitherto been generally an advocate for the
" NABOB, whose *extcrsions* and *oppressions*, I im-
" puted to the neceffity of the times, and want
" of œconomy in his revenues ; but if, &c.'s
The fpirited, juft, and pathetic conclufion of the
paragraph, you have already given.—I fet forth,
page 41. before referred to, that " The advices fent
" from DACCA, touching thefe murders, were dif-
" patched immediately on the rumour of the deed,
" and from thence, as ufual, imperfect; *fubfequent*
" *advices* brought the true ftate of the execution
" as follows :

" GOSSETA BEGUM, widow of SHAW AMET
" JUNG :

" EMNA BEGUM, mother to SURAJAH DOWLA,
" and widow to GEYNDE AMET :

" MORAD DOWLA KHAN, the fon of PATSHA
" KOOLY KHAN, adopted fon of SHAW AMET
" JUNG :

" LUTSEN NESSA BEGUM, widow of SURAJAH
" DOWLA ;

" Her infant daughter, by SURAJAH DOWLA."

The

The advices from DACCA said, these perished with about twenty of their women. Mr. VANSITTART's intelligence says, about seventy.—Mr. HASTINGS's information says, nine persons, being the whole of the family, without specifying the number of the inferior women; but all accounts agreed, that ALIVERDI's BEGUM escaped the massacre of her whole family.

Whether this charge laid against the SUBAH be true or false, I have made it sufficiently manifest it came from DACCA by express from our gentlemen there resident, on the very scene of action; the words of my letter to Mr. HASTINGS minutely corresponded with the terms of the express, without the least exaggeration; *the subsequent advices from DACCA confirmed their former intelligence,* and forwarded particulars. Mr. HASTINGS replies six days after the receipt of mine; and upon enquiry is informed, the number of the family murdered exceeds the DACCA advices:—If my veracity is doubted, regarding the express from DACCA, I appeal to WILLIAM MACGUIRE, Esq; then a member of the Select Committee, and to CULLING SMITH, Esq; then secretary to the Select Committee, both now in ENGLAND, to declare whether those advices did, or did not arrive from

DACCA

DACCA about the time, and to the purpose which I have alleged.——Indeed the rankest of my enemies would hardly believe I could be so weak, as well as wicked, to tell Mr. HASTINGS, then in the public situation of the *Company's Resident*, That " *By express yesterday from* DACCA, *we have ad-* " *vice, &c.*" if no such express and advice had been received.

On the whole I say, that supposing the charge against the SUBAH "*cruel aspersions, and void of all* " *truth*," they were no aspersions of mine; as his Lordship would have found, had he (as in equity and honour bound, before he made so free with any Gentleman's character) traced this charge to its rise.——I allow his Lordship has powerful and interesting motives for *defending* " *the honour of* JAF- " FIER ALY KHAN ;" but motives of another kind, motives of *impartial justice*, should have checked his zeal in the present instance: for as the fact stands, in place of my having asperfed the SU- BAH, his Lordship has, without any real cause or foundation, loaded *me with a cruel aspersion, void of all truth*, if (as I said before) the paragraph you give the Public from his Lordship's letter be genuine.

I have

I have hitherto proceeded on the fuppofition that this charge againft the Soubah is falfe,, but I will now beg leave to lay before the Public my reafons for ftill believing it true. In the firft place, it can hardly be conceived, that a charge fhould be fo minutely and circumftantially laid by gentlemen on the fpot,, without foundation. Secondly, the charge (heavy and cruel as it was, if not true) was never contradicted, during my ftay in India, by any advices from Dacca or elfewhere; nor fince, that I have heard, until very lately. Thirdly, For that I find Lord Clive founds his judgment and cenfure upon the addrefs to him of the 10th December, 1765, and the lift annexed to it, page 24 and 25 of your pamphlet; neither of which invalidates the charge, but only fhews his Lordfhip was deceived by here and there the fimilarity of names: but one in the lift correfponds with the names tranfmitted from Dacca, viz. Moraud Ul Dowla, who calls himfelf the fon of Jeeram Ul Dowla; whereas the Morad Dowla, mentioned in the Dacca exprefs, was inconteftably the fon of Patsha Koolee Khan. Neither the addrefs or lift make any mention of Gosseta Begum, widow of Shaw Amet Jung; nor of Emna Begum, the mother of Surajah Dowla.—The widow of Aliverdy may be living,

I

ing, fhe is faid to have efcaped the flaughter.—
The wife and daughter of SURAJAH DOWLA have
a place in the addrefs, by the name of SHOOKA
BOLLA CAWN; whereas the DACCA advices call
her LUTSEN NESSA BEGUM: SURAJAH DOWLA
probably had two wives and two daughters, which
reconciles the difference. The real fact appears to
be this, that almoft all the lift of prifoners re-
leafed by his Lordfhip are the family of SUJAH
DOWLA and SIRFERAZ KHAN, who we all know
were imprifoned many years at DACCA, and not
the family of ALIVERDY KHAN, charged by the
advices to have been cut off by JAFFIER KHAN,
in June 1760; but be they one or other, or
partly each, and be the charge againft the SU-
BAH *true* or *falfe*, it affects not me in any fhape,
as I have demonftrably proved.

Here I muft remark, that although you fet out
with impeaching my whole Memorial of *falfehood*
or *mifreprefentation in every inftance*, yet you think
proper to drop it before you have gone through
one third; for this I believe you had very co-
gent reafons.——The remainder of it you make
fhort work with; and being determined to clofe
with as little good breeding as you began, you
fay,

say, page 26. " The rest of this Memorial needs
" no comment; but here I shall observe, that
" most of what Mr. HOLWELL has published, is
" entitled to equal credit with this Memorial."
That you intended me no compliment in this con-
clusion, is pretty plain; but you inadvertently pay
me the highest you could possibly devise : for as I
have *generally*, in my Answer to the EAST INDIA
OBSERVER, N° 6. and *minutely* here, detected, ex-
posed, and refuted, beyond the reach of cavil, all
your shameful superficial attacks and insinuations
against my Memorial, I will not doubt, but from
the candor of the Public, and even from *the circle*
of your own acquaintance, I shall be entitled to an
equal degree of credit regarding my other publications ; I desire it only in proportion as I have sup-
ported *(in every instance)* my veracity in that of my
Memorial.

I now, Sir, take my leave of you——assuring
you most faithfully, that be your provocations in
future what they will, I shall never more think
you worth my notice, *in this way*, at least.

J. Z. HOLWELL.

BEENHAM-HOUSE,
BERKS, 24th Jan. 1767.

www.ingramcontent.com/pod-product-compliance
Lightning Source LLC
Chambersburg PA
CBHW031246260626
47169CB00007B/2466